A Child's
Garden of Verses

A Child's
Garden of Verses

Robert Louis Stevenson

Claremont Books
London

This edition published 1995 by Claremont Books, an
imprint of Godfrey Cave Associates, 42 Bloomsbury Street,
London, WC1B 3QJ.

ISBN 1 85471 636 0

Printed and bound by Firmin-Didot (France),
Group Herissey. No d'impression : 30190.

Biographical Note

ROBERT Louis Stevenson was born in Edinburgh in 1850, and died in Samoa in 1894. His father and grandfather were both famous engineers, the latter having designed and constructed no fewer than twenty lighthouses, including the Bell Rock. In 1871 he began to read for the Bar, and was called in 1875, but never practised. From childhood he was bent on a literary career, and when he was only sixteen his pamphlet on *The Pentland Rising* was published. His first book was *An Inland Voyage,* (1878); it was followed in 1879 by *Travels with a Donkey in the Cevennes.* Some of his contributions to the *Cornhill* and *Temple Bar* were later published in volume form as *Virginibus*

Puerisque (1881) and *Familiar Studies of Men and Books* (1882). *New Arabian Nights* appeared first in *London,* also in 1882. In 1879 he went to California, writing all the time in spite of serious illness. In 1880 he married Fanny Osbourne, and the same year returned to this country, living for a time at Bournemouth. In 1887 his father died, and he and his wife settled at Vailima in Samoa. *Treasure Island,* originally called *The Sea-Cook,* first appeared as a serial in *Young Folks* in 1882, and was his first work to make him popular. Amongst his other best-known works are *Prince Otto, The Black Arrow* (1882), *The Dynamiter, The Strange Case of Dr Jekyll and Mr Hyde* (1886), *Kidnapped* (1886), *Catriona* (1893), and *The Master of Ballantrae* (1889). In collaboration with his stepson, Lloyd Osbourne, he wrote *The Wrong Box* (1889), *The Wrecker* (1892), and *Ebb-Tide* (1894). *St Ives,* which he left unfinished, was concluded by Sir Arthur Quiller-Couch and published in 1897.

He was working on *Weir of Hermiston,* which promised to be the greatest of his books, when he died. He also wrote many poems, including those in the ever-popular *Child's Garden of Verses* which was published in 1885. Stevenson developed his exceedingly characteristic style with intense effort, and the determination with which he defied constant ill-health was heroic.

Prefatory Note

By Mrs R. L. Stevenson

DURING all the early part of her married life, Margaret Stevenson was more or less an invalid, with persistent and alarming symptoms of consumption; her only child, Robert Louis, inherited from her a predisposition to affections of the lungs. He was unfortunate, besides, in having to endure in infancy the climate of Edinburgh, which with its cold mists and penetrating east winds was far from a desirable home for a delicate child. Unable, through her own ill health, to take proper charge of her little son, his mother was forced to give him over almost entirely into the hands of hired nurses. The reign of the first nurse was very short, she being accidentally discovered in a public house much the worse for drink, while her tender charge, done up in a parcel, lay tucked out of sight on a shelf behind the bar. The second nurse proved no better, but the third, Alison Cunningham, familiarly called Cummy, proved an estimable woman, who soon won the confidence of the family.

Cummy's piety was her strongest recommendation, but her convictions and consequent teachings, believing as she did in a literal hell along with the other tenets of her church, were rather strong meat for the mental digestion of an imaginative, nervous child. My husband has told me of the terrors of the night, when he dared not go to sleep lest he should wake amid the flames of eternal torment, and how he would be taken from his bed in the morning unrefreshed, feverish, and ill, but rejoicing that he had gained at least a respite from what he believed to be his just doom; Cummy, kindly soul, never dreaming of the dire effect of her religious training. The nursery, in the custom of the time, was kept almost hermetically closed, so that not a breath of air could penetrate from the outside; if little Smoutie, as he was called, waked from his dreams with cries of fright, the watchful Cummy was ready to make him a fresh drink of coffee, which she considered a particularly soothing beverage. According to her lights she was faithful and conscientious, and the child regarded her with the deepest affection.

The terrifying aspects of religion were generally confined to the night hours. In the daytime Cummy, with her contagious gaiety and unceasing inventions for the amusement of her nursling, made the time fly on wings. Her imagination was almost as vivid as the child's, and her tact in his management was unfailing. She had a great feeling for poetry and the music of words, and can still tell a story with much dramatic effect. When the sick child turned from his food and would not eat, Cummy could usually persuade him to another effort by saying, "It is made from the finest of the wheat." The biblical words "shew bread" might also be used when everything else failed, but I fancy Cummy was chary of quoting from the sacred book unless the occasion were very serious indeed.

Had my husband's infancy been passed in the fresh air and sunshine of a milder climate, his whole life might have been different. His choice of the profession of literature was an acknowledgment that his health would not admit of his becoming what he wished to be most—a soldier. To be sure, the child often visited Colinton Manse, where the grandchildren of Dr Balfour were more than welcome. To question the healthfulness of Colinton would be like a heresy in the family, but it lies on low, damp ground, and in any other part of the world would suggest malaria. No doubt, too, the minister's little grandson would be carefully dressed to befit his position, and not allowed the freedom that would have been so wholesome for him.

Judged by the standards of today, the methods of the medical profession were inconceivably harsh and ignorant, and it seems a miracle that my husband should have survived their treatment and grown to manhood. When the little Louis was stricken with gastric fever he was dosed with powerful drugs; no one thought of looking into the sanitary condition of the premises, which were after-

wards found to have been for years in a most
dangerous state. And when the child, weak-
ened by an attack of pneumonia, took cold
after cold, antimonial wine was administered
continuously for a period extending into
months; "enough," said Dr George Balfour,
"to ruin his constitution for life." No wonder
that after a little time at play he became so
feverishly excited that his toys must be re-
moved and his playmates sent away.

My husband drew upon his memory for
The Sick Child who lay awake hoping for the
dawn, and listening for the sound of the
morning carts that proved the weary night
was almost over. Indeed, every poem in *The
Child's Garden* was a bit out of his own
childhood. He had little understanding of
children in general; I remember his watching
with puzzled amazement the games of a little
brother and sister who were visiting us at
Bournemouth. Their poverty of resource, and
the spiritless way they went about their sport,
were most distressing to him. When he found
that they were not exceptional, but repre-
sented a pretty fair average, he exclaimed: "I

see the approaching decline of England! There is something radically wrong in a generation that does not know how to play." I imagine, however, that it requires something almost like genius to play as he played, and that it was hardly fair to judge our little guests from the plane of his own childhood.

In spite of the many days and nights passed in the "Land of Counterpane", and shining, perhaps, all the brighter by comparison, there were brilliant episodes of play that remained clearer in my husband's memory than almost any other part of his life. He was especially happy in the companionship of two of his Edinburgh cousins—Willie and Henrietta Traquair. As a little girl, Henrietta already showed the characteristics that were her charm in womanhood. Never quarrelsome, and always cheerfully willing to take a secondary place, she nevertheless made her individuality felt, and threw a romantic glamour over every part she assumed. Even the wicked ogre, or giant, she endowed with unexpected attributes of generosity, and her impersonation of a chivalrous knight was ideal. When I last saw Henrietta, a few years ago, we both knew that she had but a little while to live, but the undaunted light in her eyes seemed to say:—

"Must we to bed, indeed? Well then
Let us arise and go like men."

From the memory of these early days my husband plucked a blossom here and there for *The Child's Garden*. A beginning was made by the writing of a few verses while we stopped in Braemar. A few months later, in Hyères, the games of his childhood served in a new way again to interest and amuse him. After a terrible haemorrhage, he fell a victim to sciatica, and at the same time was temporarily blind from an attack of ophthalmia. Not only was all light excluded from the room where he lay, but on account of the haemorrhage his right arm was closely bound to his side. Most men would have succumbed to the force of circumstances, but he, undismayed, determined to circumvent the fate he would not accept. Across his bed a board was laid on which large sheets of paper were pinned; on these, or on a slate fastened to the board, he laboriously wrote out in the darkness, with his left hand, many more of the songs of his childhood. In 1885 these were collected in a volume first called *Penny Whistles*, but afterwards changed to A *Child's Garden of Verses*, and published under that name with the addition of six envoys.

To Alison Cunningham

From Her Boy

FOR the long nights you lay awake
And watched for my unworthy sake:
For your most comfortable hand
That led me through the uneven land:
For all the story-books you read:
For all the pains you comforted:
For all you pitied, all you bore,
In sad and happy days of yore:—
My second Mother, my first Wife,
The angel of my infant life—
From the sick child, now well and old,
Take, nurse, the little book you hold !

And grant it, Heaven, that all who read
May find as dear a nurse at need,
And every child who lists my rhyme,
In the bright, fireside, nursery clime,
May hear it in as kind a voice
As made my childish days rejoice!

R.L.S.

Contents

A Child's Garden
of Verses

The Child Alone

Garden Days

Envoys

A CHILD'S GARDEN
OF VERSES

A Child's Garden

of Verses

1
Bed in Summer

IN winter I get up at night
And dress by yellow candle-light.
In summer, quite the other way,
I have to go to bed by day.

I have to go to bed and see
The birds still hopping on the tree,
Or hear the grown-up people's feet
Still going past me in the street.

And does it not seem hard to you,
When all the sky is clear and blue,
And I should like so much to play,
To have to go to bed by day?

2
A Thought

IT is very nice to think
The world is full of meat and drink,
With little children saying grace
In every Christian kind of place.

3
At the Seaside

WHEN I was down beside the sea
  A wooden spade they gave to me
  To dig the sandy shore.
My holes were empty like a cup,
In every hole the sea came up,
  Till it could come no more.

4
Young Night Thought

ALL night long and every night,
When my mamma puts out the light,
I see the people marching by,
As plain as day, before my eye.

Armies and emperors and kings,
All carrying different kind of things,
And marching in so grand a way,
You never saw the like by day.

So fine a show was never seen,
At the great circus on the green;
For every kind of beast and man
Is marching in that caravan.

At first they move a little slow,
But still the faster on they go,
And still beside them close I keep
Until we reach the town of Sleep.

5
Whole Duty of Children

A CHILD should always say
    what's true
And speak when he is spoken
    to,
And behave mannerly at table;
At least as far as he is able.

6
Rain

THE rain is raining all around,
It falls on field and tree,
It rains on the umbrellas here,
And on the ships at sea.

7
Pirate Story

THREE of us afloat in the meadow by
   the swing,
  Three of us aboard in the basket on the
   lea.
Winds are in the air, they are blowing in
   the spring,
  And waves are on the meadow like the
   waves there are at sea.

Where shall we adventure, to-day that
   we're afloat,
  Wary of the weather and steering by a
   star ?

Shall it be to Africa, a-steering of the
    boat,
    To Providence, or Babylon, or off to
    Malabar ?

Hi ! but here's a squadron a-rowing on
    the sea—
    Cattle on the meadow a-charging
    with a roar !
Quick, and we'll escape them, they're
    as mad as they can be,
    The wicket is the harbour and the
    garden is the shore.

8
Foreign Lands

UP into the cherry tree
Who should climb but little me ?
I held the trunk with both my hands
And looked abroad on foreign lands.

I saw the next door garden lie,
Adorned with flowers, before my eye,
And many pleasant places more
That I had never seen before.

I saw the dimpling river pass
And be the sky's blue looking-glass;
The dusty roads go up and down
With people tramping in to town.

If I could find a higher tree
Farther and farther I should see,
To where the grown-up river slips
Into the sea among the ships,

To where the roads on either hand
Lead onward into fairy land,
Where all the children dine at five,
And all the playthings come alive.

9
Windy nights

WHENEVER the moon and stars are set,
  Whenever the wind is high,
All night long in the dark and wet,
  A man goes riding by.
Late in the night when the fires are out,
Why does he gallop and gallop about ?

Whenever the trees are crying aloud,
  And ships are tossed at sea,
By, on the highway, low and loud,
  By at the gallop goes he.
By at the gallop he goes, and then
By he comes back at the gallop again.

10
Travel

I SHOULD like to rise and go
Where the golden apples grow;—
Where below another sky
Parrot islands anchored lie,
And, watched by cockatoos and goats,
Lonely Crusoes building boats,—
Where in sunshine reaching out
Eastern cities, miles about,
Are with mosque and minaret
Among sandy gardens set,
And the rich goods from near and far
Hang for sale in the bazaar;—
Where the Great Wall round China
     goes,
And on one side the desert blows,
And with bell and voice and drum,
Cities on the other hum;—

Where are forests, hot as fire,
Wide as England, tall as a spire,
Full of apes and cocoa-nuts
And the negro-hunters' huts;—
Where the knotty crocodile
Lies and blinks in the Nile,
And the red flamingo flies
Hunting fish before his eyes;—
Where in jungles, near and far,
Man-devouring tigers are,
Lying close and giving ear
Lest the hunt be drawing near,
Or a comer-by be seen
Swinging in a palanquin;—
Where among the desert sands
Some deserted city stands,
All its children, sweep and prince,
Grown to manhood ages since,
Not a foot in street or house,
Not a stir of child or mouse,

And when kindly falls the night,
In all the town no spark of light.
There I'll come when I'm a man
With a camel caravan;
Light a fire in the gloom
Of some dusty dining-room;
See the pictures on the walls,
Heroes, fights and festivals;
And in a corner find the toys
Of the old Egyptian boys.

11
Singing

OF speckled eggs the birdie sings
  And nests among the trees;
The sailor sings of ropes and things
  In ships upon the seas.

The children sing in far Japan,
  The children sing in Spain;
The organ with the organ man
  Is singing in the rain.

12
Looking Forward

WHEN I am grown to man's estate
I shall be very proud and great,
And tell the other girls and boys
Not to meddle with my toys.

13
A Good Play

WE built a ship upon the stairs
All made of the back-bedroom
     chairs,
And filled it full of sofa pillows
To go a-sailing on the billows.

We took a saw and several nails,
And water in the nursery pails;
And Tom said, 'Let us also take
An apple and a slice of cake; '—
Which was enough for Tom and
     me
To go a-sailing on, till tea.

We sailed along for days and days,
And had the very best of plays;
But Tom fell out and hurt his knee,
So there was no one left but me.

14
Where go the Boats?

DARK brown is the river,
  Golden is the sand.
It flows along for ever,
  With trees on either hand.

Green leaves a-floating,
  Castles of the foam,
Boats of mine a-boating—
  Where will all come home ?

On goes the river
  And out past the mill,
Away down the valley,
  Away down the hill.

Away down the river,
　　A hundred miles or more,
Other little children
　　Shall bring my boats ashore.

15
Auntie's Skirts

WHENEVER Auntie moves around,
Her dresses make a curious sound;
They trail behind her up the floor,
And trundle after through the door.

16
The Land of Counterpane

WHEN I was sick and lay a-bed,
I had two pillows at my head,
And all my toys beside me lay
To keep me happy all the day.

And sometimes for an hour or so
I watched my leaden soldiers go,
With different uniforms and drills,
Among the bed-clothes, through the hills

And sometimes sent my ships in fleets
All up and down among the sheets;
Or brought my trees and houses out,
And planted cities all about.

I was the giant great and still
That sits upon the pillow-hill,
And sees before him, dale and plain,
The pleasant land of counterpane.

17
The Land of Nod

FROM breakfast on all through the day
At home among my friends I stay;
But every night I go abroad
Afar into the Land of Nod.

All by myself I have to go,
With none to tell me what to do—
All alone beside the streams
And up the mountain-sides of dreams.

The strangest things are there for me,
Both things to eat and things to see,
And many frightening sights abroad
Till morning in the Land of Nod.

Try as I like to find the way,
I never can get back by day,
Nor can remember plain and clear
The curious music that I hear.

18
My Shadow

I HAVE a little shadow that goes in
     and out with me,
And what can be the use of him is
     more than I can see.
He is very, very like me from the heels
     up to the head;
And I see him jump before me, when I
     jump into my bed.

The funniest thing about him is the
     way he likes to grow—
Not at all like proper children, which
     is always very slow;
For he sometimes shoots up taller like
     an india-rubber ball,
And he sometimes gets so little that
     there's none of him at all.

He hasn't got a notion of how children
    ought to play,
And can only make a fool of me in
    every sort of way.
He stays so close beside me, he's a
    coward you can see;
I'd think shame to stick to nursie as
    that shadow sticks to me !

One morning, very early, before the
    sun was up,
I rose and found the shining dew on
    every buttercup;
But my lazy little shadow, like an
    arrant sleepy-head,
Had stayed at home behind me and
    was fast asleep in bed.

19
System

EVERY night my prayers I say,
And get my dinner every day;
And every day that I've been good,
I get an orange after food.

The child that is not clean and neat,
With lots of toys and things to eat,
He is a naughty child, I'm sure
Or else his dear papa is poor.

20
A Good Boy

I WOKE before the morning, I was
    happy all the day,
I never said an ugly word, but smiled
    and stuck to play.

And now at last the sun is going down
    behind the wood,
And I am very happy, for I know that
    I've been good.

My bed is waiting cool and fresh, with
    linen smooth and fair,
And I must off to sleepsin-by, and not
    forget my prayer.

I know that, till to-morrow I shall see
    the sun arise,
No ugly dream shall fright my mind,
    no ugly sight my eyes,

But slumber hold me tightly till I
    waken in the dawn,
And hear the thrushes singing in the
    lilacs round the lawn.

21
Escape at Bedtime

THE lights from the parlour and
  kitchen shone out
  Through the blinds and the
  windows and bars;
And high overhead and all moving
  about,
  There were thousands of millions of
  stars.
There ne'er were such thousands of
  leaves on a tree,
  Nor of people in church or the Park,
As the crowds of the stars that looked
  down upon me,
  And that glittered and winked in the
  dark.

The Dog, and the Plough, and the Hunter,
    and all,
  And the Star of the Sailor, and Mars,
These shone in the sky, and the pail by the
    wall
  Would be half full of water and stars.
They saw me at last, and they chased me
    with cries,
  And they soon had me packed into bed;
But the glory kept shining and bright in
    my eyes,
  And the stars going round in my head.

22
Marching Song

BRING the comb and play upon it !
  Marching, here we come !
Willie cocks his highland bonnet,
  Johnnie beats the drum.

Mary Jane commands the party,
  Peter leads the rear;
Feet in time, alert and hearty,
  Each a grenadier !

All in the most martial manner
  Marching double-quick;
While the napkin like a banner
  Waves upon the stick !

Here's enough of fame and pillage,
  Great commander Jane !
Now that we've been round the
    village,
  Let's go home again.

23
The Cow

THE friendly cow all red and white,
  I love with all my heart:
She gives me cream with all her
    might,
  To eat with apple-tart.

She wanders lowing here and there,
  And yet she cannot stray,
All in the pleasant open air,
  The pleasant light of day;

And blown by all the winds that pass
  And wet with all the showers,
She walks among the meadow grass
  And eats the meadow flowers.

24
Happy Thought

THE world is so full of a number of
    things,
I'm sure we should all be as happy as
    kings.

25
The Wind

I SAW you toss the kites on high
And blow the birds about the sky;
And all around I heard you pass,
Like ladies' skirts across the grass—
    O wind, a-blowing all day long,
    O wind, that sings so loud a song !

I saw the different things you did,
But always you yourself you hid.
I felt you push, I heard you call,
I could not see yourself at all—
    O wind, a-blowing all day long,
    O wind, that sings so loud a song !

O you that are so strong and cold,
O blower, are you young or old ?
Are you a beast of field and tree,
Or just a stronger child than me ?
    O wind, a-blowing all day long,
    O wind, that sings so loud a song !

26
Keepsake Mill

OVER the borders, a sin without
    pardon,
  Breaking the branches and
    crawling below,
Out through the breach in the wall of
    the garden,
  Down by the banks of the river, we
    go.

Here is the mill with the humming of
    thunder,
  Here is the weir with the wonder
    of foam,
Here is the sluice with the race
    running under—
  Marvellous places, though handy
    to home !

Sounds of the village grow stiller and
    stiller,
  Stiller the note of the birds on the hill;
Dusty and dim are the eyes of the miller,
  Deaf are his ears with the moil of the
    mill.

Years may go by, and the wheel in the
    river
  Wheel as it wheels for us, children, to-
    day,
Wheel and keep roaring and foaming for
    ever
  Long after all of the boys are away.

Home from the Indies and home from
     the ocean,
   Heroes and soldiers we all shall come
      home;
Still we shall find the old mill wheel in
     motion,
   Turning and churning that river to
      foam.

You with the bean that I gave when we
     quarrelled,
   I with your marble of Saturday last,
Honoured and old and all gaily
     apparelled,
   Here we shall meet and remember the
      past.

27
Good and bad Children

CHILDREN, you are very little,
And your bones are very brittle;
If you would grow great and
    stately,
You must try to walk sedately.

You must still be bright and quiet,
And content with simple diet;
And   remain,   through   all
    bewild'ring,
Innocent and honest children.

Happy hearts and happy faces,
Happy play in grassy places—
That was how, in ancient ages,
Children grew to kings and sages.

But the unkind and the unruly,
And the sort who eat unduly,
They must never hope for glory—
Theirs is quite a different story !

Cruel children, crying babies,
All grow up as geese and gabies,
Hated, as their age increases,
By their nephews and their nieces.

28
Foreign Children

LITTLE Indian, Sioux or Crow,
Little frosty Eskimo,
Little Turk or Japanee,
O ! don't you wish that you were me ?

You have seen the scarlet trees
And the lions over seas;
You have eaten ostrich eggs,
And turned the turtles off their legs.

Such a life is very fine,
But it's not so nice as mine:
You must often, as you trod,
Have wearied *not* to be abroad.

You have curious things to eat,
I am fed on proper meat;
You must dwell beyond the foam,
But I am safe and live at home.

   Little Indian, Sioux or Crow,
   Little frosty Eskimo,
   Little Turk or Japanee,
O ! don't you wish that you were me ?

29
The Sun's Travels

THE sun is not a-bed, when I
At night upon my pillow lie;
Still round the earth his way he
     takes,
And morning after morning makes.

While here at home, in shining day,
We round the sunny garden play,
Each little Indian sleepy-head
Is being kissed and put to bed.

And when at eve I rise from tea,
Day dawns beyond the Atlantic
     Sea,
And all the children in the West
Are getting up and being dressed.

30
The Lamplighter

MY tea is nearly ready and the sun
    has left the sky;
It's time to take the window to see
    Leerie going by;
For every night at teatime and
    before you take your seat,
With lantern and with ladder he
    comes posting up the street.

Now Tom would be a driver and
    Maria go to sea,
And my papa's a banker and as
    rich as he can be;
But I, when I am stronger and can
    choose what I'm to do,
O Leerie, I'll go round at night and
    light the lamps with you !

For we are very lucky, with a
    lamp before the door,
And Leerie stops to light it as he
    lights so many more;
And O ! before you hurry by
    with ladder and with light,
O Leerie, see a little child and
    nod to him to-night !

31
My Bed is a Boat

MY bed is like a little boat;
  Nurse helps me in when I
    embark;
She girds me in my sailor's coat
  And starts me in the dark.

At night, I go on board and say
  Good night to all my friends on
    shore;
  I shut my eyes and sail away
And see and hear no more.

  And sometimes things to bed I
    take,
As prudent sailors have to do:

Perhaps a slice of wedding-
   cake,
Perhaps a toy or two.

All night across the dark we
   steer:
But when the day returns at last
   Safe in my room, beside the
     pier,
I find my vessel fast.

32
The Moon

THE moon has a face like the clock
　　in the hall;
She shines on thieves on the garden
　　wall,
On streets and fields and harbour
　　quays,
And birdies asleep in the forks of
　　the trees.

The squalling cat and the squeaking
　　mouse.
The howling dog by the door of the
　　house,
The bat that lies in bed at noon,
All love to be out by the light of the
　　moon.

But all of the things that belong to
    the day
Cuddle to sleep to be out of her way;
And flowers and children close their
    eyes
Till up in the morning the sun shall
    arise.

33
The Swing

How do you like to go up in a swing,
   Up in the air so blue ?
Oh, I do think it the pleasantest thing
   Ever a child can do !

Up in the air and over the wall,
   Till I can see so wide,
Rivers and trees and cattle and all
   Over the countryside—

Till I look down on the garden green,
   Down on the roof so brown—
Up in the air I go flying again,
   Up in the air and down !

34
Time to Rise

A BIRDIE with a yellow bill
Hopped upon the window sill,
Cocked his shining eye and said:
' Ain't you 'shamed, you sleepy-head ? '

35
Looking-Glass River

SMOOTH it slides upon its travel,
　Here a wimple, there a gleam—
　　O the clean gravel !
　　O the smooth stream !

Sailing blossoms, silver fishes,
　Paven pools as clear as air—
　　How a child wishes
　　To live down there !

We can see our coloured faces
　Floating on the shaken pool
　　Down in cool places,
　　Dim and very cool;

Till a wind or water wrinkle,
  Dipping marten, plumping trout,
    Spreads in a twinkle
    And blots all out.

See the rings pursue each other;
  All below grows black as night,
    Just as if mother
    Had blown out the light !

Patience, children, just a minute—
  See the spreading circles die;
    The stream and all in it
    Will clear by-and-by.

36
Fairy Bread

COME up here, O dusty feet !
   Here is fairy bread to eat.
Here in my retiring room,
   Children, you may dine
On the golden smell of broom
   And the shade of pine;
And when you have eaten well,
Fairy stories hear and tell.

37
From a Railway Carriage

FASTER than fairies, faster than witches,
Bridges and houses, hedges and ditches;
And charging along like troops in a battle,
All through the meadows the horses and
    cattle:
All of the sights of the hill and the plain
Fly as thick as driving rain;
And ever again, in the wink of an eye,
Painted stations whistle by.

Here is a child who clambers and
    scrambles,
All by himself and gathering brambles;
Here is a tramp who stands and gazes;
And there is the green for stringing the
    daisies !

Here is a cart run away in the road
Lumping along with man and load;
And here is a mill and there is a river
Each a glimpse and gone for ever !

38
Winter-Time

LATE lies the wintry sun a-bed,
A frosty, fiery sleepy-head;
Blinks but an hour or two; and then,
A blood-red orange, sets again.

Before the stars have left the skies,
At morning in the dark I rise;
And shivering in my nakedness,
By the cold candle, bathe and dress.

Close by the jolly fire I sit
To warm my frozen bones a bit;
Or with a reindeer sled, explore
The colder countries round the door.

When to go out, my nurse doth wrap
Me in my comforter and cap:
The cold wind burns my face, and
    blows
Its frosty pepper up my nose.

Black are my steps on silver sod;
Thick blows my frosty breath abroad;
And tree and house, and hill and lake,
Are frosted like a wedding-cake.

39
The Hayloft

THROUGH all the pleasant meadow-
    side
  The grass grew shoulder-high,
Till the shining scythes went far and
    wide
  And cut it down to dry.

These green and sweetly smelling
    crops
  They led in waggons home;
And they piled them here in mountain
    tops
  For mountaineers to roam.

Here is Mount Clear, Mount Rusty-Nail,
  Mount Eagle and Mount High;—
The mice that in these mountains dwell,
  No happier are than I !

O what a joy to clamber there,
  O what a place for play,
With the sweet, the dim, the dusty air,
  The happy hills of hay.

40
Farewell to the Farm

THE coach is at the door at last;
The eager children, mounting fast
And kissing hands, in chorus sing:
Good-bye, good-bye, to everything !

To house and garden, field and lawn,
The meadow-gates we swang upon,
To pump and stable, tree and swing,
Good-bye, good-bye, to everything !

And fare you well for evermore,
O ladder at the hayloft door,
O hayloft where the cobwebs cling,
Good-bye, good-bye, to everything !

Crack goes the whip, and off we go;
The trees and houses smaller grow;
Last, round the woody turn we
    swing:
Good-bye, good-bye, to everything !

41
North-West Passage

1 Good Night

WHEN the bright lamp is carried in,
The sunless hours again begin;
O'er all without, in field and lane,
The haunted night returns again.

Now we behold the embers flee
About the firelit hearth; and see
Our faces painted as we pass,
Like pictures, on the window-glass.

Must we to bed indeed ? Well then,
Let us arise and go like men,
And face with an undaunted tread
The long black passage up to bed.

Farewell, O brother, sister, sire !
O pleasant party round the fire !
The songs you sing, the tales you tell,
Till far to-morrow, fare ye well !

2 Shadow March

ALL round the house is the jet-
    black night;
  It stares through the window-
    pane;
It crawls in the corners, hiding from
    the light,
  And it moves with the moving
    flame.

Now my little heart goes a-beating
    like a drum,
  With the breath of the Bogie in
    my hair;
And all round the candle the
    crooked shadows come
  And go marching along up the
    stair.

The   shadow   of   the   balusters,   the
   shadow of the lamp,
  The shadow of the child that goes to
   bed—
All the wicked shadows coming, tramp,
   tramp, tramp,
  With the black night overhead.

3 In Port

LAST, to the chamber where I lie
My fearful footsteps patter nigh,
And come from out the cold and gloom
Into my warm and cheerful room.

There, safe arrived, we turn about
To keep the coming shadows out,
And close the happy door at last
On all the perils that we past.

Then, when mamma goes by to bed,
She shall come in with tiptoe tread,
And see me lying warm and fast
And in the Land of Nod at last.

THE CHILD ALONE

THE CHILD ALONE

1
The Unseen Playmate

WHEN children are playing alone on
  the green,
In comes the playmate that never was
  seen.
When children are happy and lonely and
  good,
The Friend of the Children comes out of
  the wood.

Nobody heard him and nobody saw,
His is a picture you never could draw,
But he's sure to be present, abroad or at
    home,
When children are happy and playing
    alone.

He lies in the laurels, he runs on the
    grass,
He sings when you tinkle the musical
    glass;
Whene'er you are happy and cannot tell
    why,
The Friend of the Children is sure to be
    by !

He loves to be little, he hates to be big,
'Tis he that inhabits the caves that you
   dig;
'Tis he when you play with your
   soldiers of tin
That sides with the Frenchmen and
   never can win.

'Tis he, when at night you go off to
   your bed,
Bids you go to your sleep and not
   trouble your head;
For wherever they're lying, in
   cupboard or shelf,
'Tis he will take care of your
   playthings himself !

2
My Ship and I

O IT'S I that am the captain of a tidy
    little ship,
  Of a ship that goes a-sailing on the
    pond;
And my ship it keeps a-turning all
    around and all about;
But when I'm a little older, I shall find
    the secret out
  How to send my vessel sailing on
    beyond.

For I mean to grow as little as the dolly
    at the helm,
  And the dolly I intend to come alive;
And with him beside to help me, it's a-
    sailing I shall go,

It's a-sailing on the water, when
    the jolly breezes blow
  And the vessel goes a divie-
    divie dive.

O it's then you'll see me sailing
    through the rushes and the
    reeds,
  And you'll hear the water
    singing at the prow;
For beside the dolly sailor, I'm to
    voyage and explore,
To land upon the island where no
    dolly was before,
  And to fire the penny cannon in
    the bow.

3
My Kingdom

DOWN by a shining water well
I found a very little dell,
　　No higher than my head.
The heather and the gorse about
In summer bloom were coming out,
　　Some yellow and some red.

I called the little pool a sea;
The little hills were big to me;
　　For I am very small.
I made a boat, I made a town,
I searched the caverns up and down,
　　And named them one and all.

And all about was mine, I said,
The little sparrows overhead,

The little minnows too.
This was the world and I was king;
For me the bees came by to sing,
    For me the swallows flew.

I played there were no deeper seas,
Nor any wider plains than these,
    Nor other kings than me.
At last I heard my mother call
Out from the house at evenfall,
    To call me home to tea.

And I must rise and leave my dell,
And leave my dimpled water well,
    And leave my heather blooms.
Alas ! and as my home I neared,
How very big my nurse appeared,
    How great and cool the rooms !

4
Picture-Books in Winter

SUMMER fading, winter comes—
Frosty mornings, tingling thumbs,
Window robins, winter rooks,
And the picture story-books.

Water now is turned to stone
Nurse and I can walk upon;
Still we find the flowing brooks
In the picture story-books.

All the pretty things put by,
Wait upon the children's eye,
Sheep and shepherds, trees and crooks,
In the picture story-books.

We may see how all things are,
Seas and cities, near and far,
And the flying fairies' looks,
In the picture story-books.

How am I to sing your praise,
Happy chimney-corner days,
Sitting safe in nursery nooks,
Reading picture story-books?

5
My Treasures

THESE nuts, that I keep in the back of
    the nest
Where all my lead soldiers are lying at
    rest,
Were gathered in autumn by nursie
    and me
In a wood with a well by the side of
    the sea.

This whistle we made (and how
    clearly it sounds !)
By the side of a field at the end of the
    grounds.
Of a branch of a plane, with a knife of
    my own,
It was nursie who made it, and nursie
    alone !

The stone, with the white and the
 yellow and grey,
We discovered I cannot tell *how*
 far away;
And I carried it back although
 weary and cold,
For though father denies it, I'm
 sure it is gold.

But of all of my treasures the last
 is the king,
For there's very few children
 possess such a thing;
And that is a chisel, both handle
 and blade,
Which a man who was really a
 carpenter made.

6
Block City

WHAT are you able to build with
your blocks ?
Castles and palaces, temples and
docks.
Rain may keep raining, and others
go roam,
But I can be happy and building at
home.

Let the sofa be mountains, the
carpet be sea,
There I'll establish a city for me:
A kirk and a mill and a palace
beside,
And a harbour as well where my
vessels may ride.

Great is the palace with pillar and
    wall,
A sort of a tower on the top of it
    all,
And steps coming down in an
    orderly way
To where my toy vessels lie safe
    in the bay.

This one is sailing and that one is
    moored:
Hark to the song of the sailors on
    board !
And see on the steps of my
    palace, the kings
Coming and going with presents
    and things !

Now I have done with it,
    down let it go !
All in a moment the town is
    laid low.
Block upon block lying
    scattered and free,
What is there left of my town
    by the sea ?

Yet as I saw it, I see it again,
The kirk and the palace, the
    ships and the men,
And as long as I live and
    where'er I may be,
I'll always remember my
    town by the sea.

7
The Land of Story-Books

AT evening when the lamp is
 lit,
Around the fire my parents
 sit;
They sit at home and talk and
 sing,
And do not play at anything.

Now, with my little gun, I
 crawl
All in the dark along the wall,
And follow round the forest
 track
Away behind the sofa back.

There, in the night, where
    none can spy,
All in my hunter's camp I lie,
And play at books that I have
    read
Till it is time to go to bed.

These are the hills, these are
    the woods,
These are my starry solitudes;
And there the river by whose
    brink
The roaring lions come to
    drink.

I see the others far away
As if in firelit camp they lay,
And I, like to an Indian scout,
Around their party prowled
    about.

So, when my nurse comes
    in for me,
Home I return across the
    sea,
And go to bed with
    backward looks
At my dear land of Story-
    books.

8
Armies in the Fire

THE lamps now glitter down the
    street;
Faintly sound the falling feet;
And the blue even slowly falls
About the garden trees and walls.

Now in the falling of the gloom
The red fire paints the empty room:
And warmly on the roof it looks,
And flickers on the backs of books.

Armies march by tower and spire
Of cities blazing, in the fire;—
Till as I gaze with staring eyes,
The armies fade, the lustre dies.

Then once again the glow returns;
Again the phantom city burns;
And down the red-hot valley, lo !
The phantom armies marching go !

Blinking embers, tell me true
Where are those armies marching to,
And what the burning city is
That crumbles in your furnaces !

9
The Little Land

WHEN at home alone I sit
And am very tired of it,
I have just to shut my eyes
To go sailing through the skies—
To go sailing far away
To the pleasant Land of Play;
To the fairy land afar
Where the Little People are;
Where the clover-tops are trees,
And the rain-pools are the seas,
And the leaves like little ships
Sail about on tiny trips;
And above the daisy tree
    Through the grasses,
High o'erhead the Bumble Bee
    Hums and passes.

In that forest to and fro
I can wander, I can go;
See the spider and the fly,
And the ants go marching by
Carrying parcels with their
    feet
Down the green and grassy
    street.
I can in the sorrel sit
Where the ladybird alit.
I can climb the jointed grass;
  And on high
See the greater swallows pass
  In the sky,
And the round sun rolling by
Heeding no such things as I.

Through that forest I can pass
Till, as in a looking-glass,

Humming fly and daisy tree
And my tiny self I see,
Painted very clear and neat
On the rain-pool at my feet.
Should a leaflet come to land
Drifting near to where I stand,
Straight I'll board that tiny boat
Round the rain-pool sea to float.

Little thoughtful creatures sit
On the grassy coasts of it;
Little things with lovely eyes
See me sailing with surprise.
Some are clad in armour green—
(These have sure to battle been !)—
Some are pied with ev'ry hue,
Black and crimson, gold and blue;
Some have wings and swift are gone;—
But they all look kindly on.

When my eyes I once again
Open, and see all things plain;
High bare walls, great bare floor;
Great big knobs on drawer and door;
Great big people perched on chairs,
Stitching tucks and mending tears,
Each a hill that I could climb,
And talking nonsense all the time—
  O dear me,
  That I could be
A sailor on the rain-pool sea,
A climber in the clover tree,
And just come back, a sleepy-head,
Late at night to go to bed.

GARDEN DAYS

GARDEN DAYS

1
Night And Day

WHEN the golden day is done,
  Through the closing portal,
Child and garden, flower and sun,
  Vanish all things mortal.

As the blinding shadows fall,
  As the rays diminish,
Under evening's cloak, they all
  Roll away and vanish.

Garden darkened, daisy shut,
  Child in bed, they slumber—
Glow-worm in the highway rut,
  Mice among the lumber.

In the darkness houses shine,
  Parents move with candles;
Till on all, the night divine
  Turns the bedroom handles.

Till at last the day begins
  In the east a-breaking,
In the hedges and the whins
  Sleeping birds a-waking.

In the darkness shapes of things,
  Houses, trees, and hedges,
Clearer grow; and sparrow's wings
  Beat on window ledges.

These shall wake the yawning maid;
   She the door shall open—
Finding dew on garden glade
And the morning broken.

There my garden grows again
   Green and rosy painted,
As at eve behind the pane
   From my eyes it fainted.

Just as it was shut away,
   Toy-like, in the even,
Here I see it glow with day
   Under glowing heaven.

Every path and every plot,
   Every bush of roses,
Every blue forget-me-not
   Where the dew reposes,

' Up ! ' they cry, ' the day is come
  On the smiling valleys;
We have beat the morning drum;
  Playmate, join your allies ! '

2
Nest Eggs

BIRDS all the sunny day
　Flutter and quarrel
Here in the arbour-like
　Tent of the laurel.

Here in the fork
　The brown nest is seated;
Four little blue eggs
　The mother keeps heated.

While we stand watching her,
　Staring like gabies,
Safe in each egg are the
　Bird's little babies.

Soon the frail eggs they shall
　Chip, and upspringing

Make all the April woods
    Merry with singing.

Younger than we are,
    O children, and frailer,
Soon in blue air they'll be,
    Singer and sailor.

We, so much older,
    Taller and stronger,
We shall look down on the
    Birdies no longer.

They shall go flying
    With musical speeches
High overhead in the
    Tops of the beeches.

In spite of our wisdom
    And sensible talking,
We on our feet must go
    Plodding and walking.

3
The Flowers

ALL the names I know from nurse:
Gardener's garters, Shepherd's purse,
Bachelor's buttons, Lady's smock,
And the Lady Hollyhock.

Fairy places, fairy things,
Fairy woods where the wild bee wings,
Tiny trees for tiny dames—
These must all be fairy names !

Tiny woods below whose boughs
Shady fairies weave a house;
Tiny tree-tops, rose or thyme,
Where the braver fairies climb !

Fair are grown-up people's trees,
But the fairest woods are these;
Where if I were not so tall,
I should live for good and all.

4
Summer Sun

GREAT is the sun, and wide he goes
Through empty heaven without repose:
And in the blue and glowing days
More thick than rain he showers his
    rays.

Though closer still the blinds we pull
To keep the shady parlour cool,
Yet he will find a chink or two
To slip his golden fingers through.

The dusty attic spider-clad
He, through the keyhole, maketh glad;
And through the broken edge of tiles,
Into the laddered hayloft smiles.

Meantime his golden face around
He bares to all the garden ground,
And sheds a warm and glittering look
Among the ivy's inmost nook.

Above the hills, along the blue,
Round the bright air with footing true
To please the child, to paint the rose,
The gardener of the World, he goes.

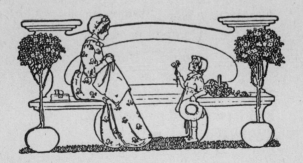

5
The Dumb Soldier

WHEN the grass was closely mown,
Walking on the lawn alone,
In the turf a hole I found
And hid a soldier underground.

Spring and daisies came apace;
Grasses hide my hiding-place;
Grasses run like a green sea
O'er the lawn up to my knee.

Under grass alone he lies,
Looking up with leaden eyes,
Scarlet coat and pointed gun,
To the stars and to the sun.

When the grass is ripe like grain,
When the scythe is stoned again,
When the lawn is shaven clear,
Then my hole shall reappear.

I shall find him, never fear,
I shall find my grenadier;
But for all that's gone and come,
I shall find my soldier dumb.

He has lived, a little thing,
In the grassy woods of spring;
Done, if he could tell me true,
Just as I should like to do.

He has seen the starry hours
And the springing of the flowers;
And the fairy things that pass
In the forests of the grass.

In the silence he has heard
Talking bee and ladybird,
And the butterfly has flown,
O'er him as he lay alone.

Not a word will he disclose,
Not a word of all he knows.
I must lay him on the shelf,
And make up the tale myself.

6
Autumn Fires

IN the other gardens
  And all up the vale,
From the autumn bonfires
  See the smoke trail !

Pleasant summer over
  And all the summer flowers,
The red fire blazes,
  The grey smoke towers.

Sing a song of seasons !
  Something bright in all !
Flowers in the summer,
  Fires in the fall !

7
The Gardener

THE gardener does not love to talk,
He makes me keep the gravel walk;
And when he puts his tools away,
He locks the door and takes the key.

Away behind the currant row
Where no one else but cook may go,
Far in the plots, I see him dig,
Old and serious, brown and big.

He digs the flowers, green, red, and
    blue,
Nor wishes to be spoken to.
He digs the flowers and cuts the hay
And never seems to want to play.

Silly gardener ! summer goes,
And winter comes with pinching toes,
When in the garden bare and brown
You must lay your barrow down.

Well now, and while the summer stays,
To profit by these garden days,
O how much wiser you would be
To play at Indian wars with me !

8
Historical Associations

DEAR Uncle Jim, this garden ground
That now you smoke your pipe around,
Has seen immortal actions done
And valiant battles lost and won.

Here we had best on tiptoe tread,
While I for safety march ahead,
For this is that enchanted ground
Where all who loiter slumber sound.

Here is the sea, here is the sand,
Here is simple Shepherd's Land,
Here are the fairy hollyhocks,
And there are Ali Baba's rocks.

But yonder, see ! apart and high,
Frozen Siberia lies; where I,
With Robert Bruce and William Tell,
Was bound by an enchanter's spell.

There, then, awhile in chains we lay,
In wintry dungeons, far from day;
But ris'n at length, with might and main,
Our iron fetters burst in twain.

Then all the horns were blown in town;
And to the ramparts clanging down,
All the giants leaped to horse
And charged behind us through the gorse.

On we rode, the others and I,
Over the mountains blue, and by
The Silver River, the sounding sea,
And the robber woods of Tartary.

A thousand miles we galloped fast,
And down the witches' lane we passed,
And rode amain, with brandished sword,
Up to the middle, through the ford.

Last we drew rein—a weary three—
Upon the lawn, in time for tea,
And from our steeds alighted down
Before the gates of Babylon.

ENVOYS

ENVOYS

1
To Willie and Henrietta

IF two may read aright
These rhymes of old delight
And house and garden play,
You two, my cousins, and you only, may.

You in a garden green
With me were king and queen,
Were hunter, soldier, tar,
And all the thousand things that children are.

Now in the elders' seat
We rest with quiet feet,
And from the window-bay
We watch the children, our successors, play.

'Time was,' the golden head
Irrevocably said;
But time which none can bind,
While flowing fast away, leaves love behind.

2
To my Mother

YOU too, my mother, read my rhymes
For love of unforgotten times,
And you may chance to hear once more
The little feet along the floor.

3
To Auntie

CHIEF of our aunts—not only I,
But all your dozen of nurslings cry—
What did the other children do ?
And what were childhood, wanting you ?

4
To Minnie

THE red room with the giant bed
Where none but elders laid their head;
The little room where you and I
Did for awhile together lie
And, simple suitor, I your hand
In decent marriage did demand;
The great day nursery, best of all,
With pictures pasted on the wall
And leaves upon the blind—
A pleasant room wherein to wake
And hear the leafy garden shake
And rustle in the wind—
And pleasant there to lie in bed
And see the pictures overhead—
The wars about Sebastopol,
The grinning guns along the wall,
The daring escalade,

The plunging ships, the bleating sheep,
The happy children ankle-deep
And laughing as they wade:
All these are vanished clean away,
And the old manse is changed to-day;
It wears an altered face
And shields a stranger race.
The river, on from mill to mill,
Flows past our childhood's garden still;
But ah ! we children never more
Shall watch it from the water-door !
Below the yew—it still is there—
Our phantom voices haunt the air
As we were still at play,
And I can hear them call and say:
' How far is it to Babylon ? '

Ah, far enough, my dear,
Far, far enough from here—
Yet you have farther gone !

' Can I get there by candle-light ? '
So goes the old refrain.
I do not know—perchance you might—
But only, children, hear it right,
Ah, never to return again !
The eternal dawn, beyond a doubt,
Shall break on hill and plain,
And put all stars and candles out,
Ere we be young again.

To you in distant India, these
I send across the seas,
Nor count it far across.
For which of us forgets
The Indian cabinets,
The bones of antelope, the wings of albatross,
The pied and painted birds and beans,
The junks and bangles, beads and screens,
The gods and sacred bells,
And the loud-humming, twisted shells ?
The level of the parlour floor

Was honest, homely, Scottish shore;
But when we climbed upon a chair,
Behold the gorgeous East was there !
Be this a fable; and behold
Me in the parlour as of old,
And Minnie just above me set
In the quaint Indian cabinet !
Smiling and kind, you grace a shelf
Too high for me to reach myself.
Reach down a hand, my dear, and take
These rhymes for old acquaintance' sake.

5
To my Name-Child

I

SOME day soon this rhyming volume, if you
    learn with proper speed,
Little Louis Sanchez, will be given you to
    read.
Then shall you discover, that your name was
    printed down
By the English printers, long before, in
    London town.

In the great and busy city where the East and
    West are met,
All the little letters did the English printer
    set;

While you thought of nothing, and were still
    too young to play,
Foreign people thought of you in places far
    away.

Ay, and while you slept, a baby, over all the
    English lands
Other little children took the volume in their
    hands;
Other children questioned, in their homes
    across the seas:
Who was little Louis, won't you tell us,
    mother, please ?

2

Now that you have spelt your lesson, lay it
    down and go and play,
Seeking shells and seaweed on the sands of
    Monterey,
Watching all the mighty whalebones, lying
    buried by the breeze,
Tiny sandy-pipers, and the huge Pacific seas.

And remember in your playing, as the seafog
    rolls to you,
Long ere you could read it, how I told you
    what to do;
And that while you thought of no one, nearly
    half the world away
Some one thought of Louis on the beach of
    Monterey !

6
To Any Reader

AS from the house your mother sees
You playing round the garden trees
So you may see, if you will look
Through the windows of this book,
Another child, far, far away,
And in another garden, play.
But do not think you can at all,
By knocking on the window, call
That child to hear you. He intent
Is all on his play-business bent.
He does not hear; he will not look,
Nor yet be lured out of this book.
For, long ago, the truth to say,
He has grown up and gone away,
And it is but a child of air
That lingers in the garden there.